Unassisted Living

Michael Jasper

UNWRECKED PRESS

Also by Michael Jasper

Unassisted Living

Even if it was his idea, JB had to admit that the kickball game in the nursing home gym was pure brilliance.

The way he figured it, the game got the old folks up and moving, it got their blood flowing, and it encouraged teamwork among the residents of Whispering Pines Rest Home. He didn't have to do much talking to convince Bart the therapist to agree to the game; Bart was always very open to suggestion when he had a hangover.

The game also gave JB a chance to kick the hell out of the ball. He didn't care one bit that he was the youngest person playing the game—by a good thirty-five years.

Eighty-five-year-old Nelly knew how to serve up a perfect pitch for kicking, and JB planned on tying the game with the ball that was now rolling his way.

So he kicked it. Hard.

As the ball bounced off the far wall of the big, windowless room that they used for therapy—and half a dozen men and woman over the age of seventy shuffled after the bouncing red ball—JB stepped on the phone book they were using for first base and charged toward the pizza box that was second base.

This is it, he thought. The tide is turning. At last.

"Safe at second!" he called out, breathlessly. Standing on the grease-stained square of cardboard, he clapped until his hands stung. "What a kick! Nice pitch, Nelly. It's rally time, folks! Rally time!"

JB waved at his elderly teammates near home plate (a used toupee that Bart the therapist had found under some folding chairs). Most of them were black, and all of them looked exhausted, but happy. The game had last nearly thirty minutes now.

This was good, JB thought. No, it was *great*. They'd remember this game, forever.

In the three minutes that had passed since JB's kick, ninety-something Abe had been making his snail-like way toward home plate behind his battered silver walker. At last the skinny old man was ready.

"All right!" JB called out from second. "We're only down by one, Abe. Kick it all the way down to Myrtle Beach! Get ready, Bart!"

Bart the therapist, a burly black man in khakis and a blue golf shirt, sat hunched over in a folding chair by first base. He was busy texting on his phone, and he ignored JB's warning just as he'd ignored most of the game.

From the "pitcher's mound," Nelly, a spry black woman with close-cropped white hair, gently rolled the kickball toward Abe. JB held his breath until Abe "kicked" the ball with his walker.

Then he charged toward home, while Abe began a slow and squeaky journey to first, his walker scraping the floor with every other step.

"I hate..." Abe panted, "this... fricking game."

JB barely heard him as he slapped the seat of the folding chair they were using as third base. He turned toward home. In the meantime, Nelly reached down to pick the ball that Abe kicked.

JB laughed and shook his head as he thundered toward home.

"Not today, Nelly," he shouted.

But then, instead of lobbing the ball at JB to try to hit him for the out, Nelly decided to tag him out. Big mistake. Air hissed in through a dozen pairs of dentures in shock as Nelly blocked home plate with her tiny body.

"Bring it, sonny boy," Nelly said with a smile.

Abe was still only halfway to first, pushing his walker at a snail's speed.

"Knock her... block off... kid," he panted.

JB was fifteen feet from Nelly and closing fast.

"I ain't stoppin'!" he shouted.

From somewhere in the back of his mind, he heard Bart the therapist calling his name.

Nelly was so small. So frail. And she was right in JB's way.

In an instant, JB's eyes changed from determined to dead. It was the look of someone who has given up. Someone who never got to be the hero of the big game.

At the last possible instant, instead of running her over, he pivoted hard around Nelly and the ball. And a loud *popping* came from his knee.

From the direction of first base, JB heard an old man's voice as if in a dream. It was Abe, saying, "Oooh. I know that sound."

JB tried to dive toward home, but his knee wouldn't cooperate. Nelly leaned down and tagged him with the ball.

"Yer *out*, youngster," she said with a grin.

Making sympathetic noises as they approach, the other white-haired players gathered around their fallen teammate. Nobody risked a hip helping him up. They saved that for Bart.

"JB!" the therapist shouted as he stomped up to him next to home base. "You *always* overdo it, man. Back to your rooms, people. Therapy hour is officially over."

After he got the old folks headed for the exit, Bart reached down to help JB to his feet with a good bit of effort. JB straightened his knee with another *pop*. All the departing elderly folks winced and groaned at the sound.

Holding his knee and grimacing, JB met Bart's gaze and took a quick, painful breath.

"We don't need to mention this to anyone in upper management, now, do we, Bart? Buddy?"

Bart just glared at JB. This sort of thing had happened before. A lot. JB figured Bart was remembering each time, and the fallout from every incident. He hoped Bart would be generous in his memories.

Finally, Bart clapped him on the back in a half-friendly, half-hostile way.

"For *you*, my man, we can make an exception. We always have, right?"

JB gave Bart a weak smile, and that look of utter defeat returned to his eyes. He began limping toward the exit as well, gritting his teeth against the pain in his knee.

"Hey," Bart said. "Need help getting back?"

"Nah," he said over his shoulder to Bart. He limped a bit faster, grimacing with pain, but he still couldn't catch up to the old folks leaving the tiny gym.

"You sure?"

"Yeah..."

JB heard Bart mutter something about "another successful therapy session."

At last he made it into the hall. He turned right and limped past four pairs of doors, one on either side of him. At last he arrived at room 25.

JB stood up as straight as his aching, thirty-six-year-old body would allow him, and then he hobbled into the room where he'd chosen to live out his early retirement.

He closed the door behind him and locked it with a soft click.

For JB, recovery started on his back.

He lay flat on the uncarpeted floor in the space between the bed and the desk, with his eyes closed, a wet washcloth on his forehead, and a pillow under his bad knee.

This room, like all rooms at the Home, was small and mostly empty, which made it easy for JB keep it neat and clean. It also kept him from wanting to stay there any longer than he absolutely had to.

But for now, he had to recover from blowing out his knee.

Thoughts, regrets, and memories—harsh memories—tapped on his temples, like ghosts haunting an old house. He refused to let any of them in.

Instead, he began talking to himself, like a yogi repeating a mantra:

"No time like the present. In the moment. Right now. No time—"

When he stopped for breath, he sat up with a groan and scoped out his room.

There was his perfectly made next to the window with the blinds drawn, as usual. Over there was the unforgiving wooden chair resting in front of his desk. And to his right was the open bathroom door. Every wall was beige and bare, and dead space filled the areas where—in the typical room of a typical person— pictures and mementos of the past would rest.

That was long enough, JB told himself. Enough wallowing in self-pity and suffering. No time like the present.

He leapt to his feet, energized. He swiped at his face with the washcloth, tossed it into the bathroom, and then stepped to the door. His limp was gone.

Everything was better, because he now had a *plan.*

Got work to do today, he thought. No time to waste. And we've got our big trip tomorrow, too.

Before walking out, JB took one look over his shoulder at the room. His eyes went blank, just for an instant, just like they did near the end of the kickball game.

With a loud click, he turned the doorknob and opened the door. He peeked to his left and froze when he spotted head nurse Reena, a black woman of about thirty-five, about seven doors down and walking away from him.

JB waited for her to disappear into a fellow resident's room. He and Reena had developed a history in the six months since his arrival here, and not much of it was good.

After a few more seconds, he exhaled and relaxed, only to run into the janitor, Peterson, a young white guy with long hair and baggy jeans. JB jumped, surprised.

Peterson, wielding his push broom like a weapon, gave JB an aggressive look from under his shaggy blond locks.

"We on for tonight, J? I gotta be out of here early to meet my AA sponsor, so... You got my back?"

JB made a face. "Just this one last time. That's it, then I'm done. This stuff is interfering with my work here."

Peterson gave JB a knowing look.

"Right, man. *Riiight.* Get back to your work, J."

JB shot a dirty look at the janitor's back as Peterson swept up the hall. Then he tiptoed across the hall to Miss Amelia's room.

Once he was inside, inhaling the slightly stale air of her room, he had to look closely to see the tiny black woman. She was almost hidden in her bed, thanks to all the machines and IVs that had been hooked up to her to keep her alive.

As usual, Amelia's eyes were closed. Her machines beeped and whirred, making it seem like there was another entity in the room with her. Something non-human and almost predatory.

JB's face remained unreadable as he watched her, waiting for a reaction.

After a few seconds of hopeful watching, he nodded, winked, and smiled.

"Maybe tomorrow, Miss Amelia. Maybe tomorrow. You take care, now."

Back in the hallway, he looked at one door, then another, and finally went to another, seemingly at random. He knocked.

A deep male voice answered, sharply, "Who's that?"

JB crossed his fingers and pushed partway into Marvin's room. He gave the old black man, who was still sturdy and imposing despite his advanced years and deteriorating faculties, a big and reassuring grin.

"We had an appointment, Mr. Stone, sir. Just a few minutes of your time."

Dressed in a wrinkled, dark blue shirt and a sharply knitted white tie, Mr. Marvin Stone waved JB over to the desk by the window. An empty chair sat waiting for JB on the other side of the desk, giving the tidy room the feel of an office.

As they shook hands, Marvin gave JB an appraising look, as if he didn't quite trust this young white fellow in his space. After listening to Marvin's stories for the past few months, JB could safely say that he didn't blame Marvin for that edge of racism. Marvin had lived a hard life.

"Ah, yes," Marvin said, all professionalism and smiles now. "You're my 10:15. Right on time. Wonderful, just wonderful."

JB smoothly picked up a yellow legal pad from the desk and sat down, playing the role of an intent reporter. This approach usually worked best with Marvin.

"Shall we pick up where we left off, Mr. Stone?"

"Oh, yes. And please, call me Marvin."

Marvin fussed with his tie and then rubbed his forehead as if he were getting a migraine. His eyes clouded over as he tried to remember.

"So where did we leave off again?"

JB noisily flipped through the blank pages of the pad.

"The day you got your company off the ground." JB looked up from the pad, as if quoting from it. The stories were the key, he knew. Each one as fascinating as the next. "One of the best days of your life, you called it."

Marvin clapped his big hands together and nodded, his brown eyes clear again.

"Of course. I showed all those doubters we had the right stuff for big business. I had to knock some heads together in downtown Durham every now and then, of course, but it had to be done."

Marvin leaned back in his chair, a hint of a smile on his face.

JB nodded and feigned note-taking with his pen-less hand.

"That's how you did it back then, son. You found a need and then you came up with a way to meet that need. For us, it was tearing down houses and using what we could from the wreckage. We left no stone unturned. Nothing wasted."

"Um-hmm," JB said, sensing Marvin's motor slowing already. "Right. Excellent."

"Don't forget," Marvin added, "the part about no stone, um. Ah. No stone... Like my name, you see. And the name of my company. No stone..."

JB paused, eyes averted, giving Marvin time to pull his memories back together.

But it was too late. Marvin went silent and started messing with his tie. He started to deflate, slumping down in his chair.

He now looked up and eyed JB suspiciously. "How did *you* get in here?"

"It's okay, Marvin—Mr. Stone. Everything's fine."

Sensing a storm about to hit, JB got up and casually headed for the door. This wasn't the first time this sort of thing had happened.

Marvin glared after him, holding the empty legal pad in one shaking hand.

"Who let *you* in?" the old man shouted at JB.

JB gritted his teeth together to keep from saying anything else and making Marvin's confusion worse. He slipped out the door and closed it behind him as softly as he could. Back in the hall, he rested his back against Marvin's door, cringing at the sound of the old man now yelling inside.

"Where's my pen? Where's my *secretary*, dammit?"

He'll be better in a few minutes, JB told himself. I hope.

Determined to continue his chats, he tiptoed down the hall towards another room. He made it about ten feet before sharp, fast footsteps stopped him. He knew those footsteps all too well.

He turned with a nervous smile and faced nurse Reena. She was almost the same age as JB, but she seemed older because of her authority and her responsibilities here at the Home. Or maybe it was just because she never smiled.

"You went in there *again*?" Reena said in a harsh whisper. "Come *on*, Mr. Beckwith. You can't keep doing this. His blood pressure alone is reason not to—"

"Please. It's JB. And I was just—"

Reena glared him into submission. JB closed his mouth with a snap and aimed a quivering thumb at the closed door of his room.

"I'll just get back to my room now..." he said meekly.

"*Excellent* idea, Mr. Beckwith."

From inside Marvin's room came a roar of frustration, followed by, "Where the goddamn hell are all my *pens*?"

JB glanced at Marvin's door and started for his own room. He stopped for a second, wanting to say something more to Reena—an apology, something, anything—but a sharp pain in his injured knee took the words from his mouth. All he could do was give a soft hiss of pain.

Reena gave him a cool look as he limped across the hall. "You should get some rest, Mr. Beckwith. Let that knee heal. Spring will be here soon, and you'll want to *get out* and take in some fresh air, I'm sure."

His hand on the door to his own room, JB couldn't help but try for the last word. It was a bad, bad habit of his. "Sure. You're the head nurse. You know best. I'll do that."

"I'm the nursing *director*, Mr. Beckwith. Think of LaTanya here as the head nurse. And here she comes with Mr. Stone's blood pressure meds. Meds he wouldn't need if you hadn't disturbed him. Again."

Leaning against his door, JB nodded slowly, chastised. She was always best at getting in the parting shot.

Reena was already walking off to meet LaTanya, a slim black woman carrying a small cup of pills. LaTanya gave JB a look like she'd like to smack him.

He nodded at both nurses, aiming for a casual tone. As if he wasn't an inmate of his own choosing, and these two weren't his jailers, more or less.

"I'll just, um, go back to my room. So I can get some healing going on. You know how it is."

"You do that," Reena said without even looking his way.

JB paused outside his room, wondering if he could sneak in one more visit with a fellow resident without Reena noticing. But Reena spotted him and shook her head once: No way.

JB opened the door and clumped back into his empty, bland room. He leaned against the door, and then his bad knee gave out. He slid heavily down to the floor. Again.

"Yeah," he whispered to himself and nobody. "My bad."

He rubbed his face and thought of his brief chat, and a smile crossed his face.

"Marvin was there, though," he said softly. "Just for a second. I had him remembering. 'No stone unturned.' Awesome. Just like his name..."

With a heavy sigh, JB shook his head, and he closed his eyes.

O nce again, JB finds himself on the floor. This time he's between *two* desks: one completely empty, and the other covered in papers, folders, bills. He searches through the paperwork spilled around him on the floor, getting more agitated with each passing second. Sunlight streams in from the window in front of him. Springtime in suburbia unfolds on the other side of the glass: kids on bikes, moms chatting on front porches, hands waving from car windows.

JB stops, looks up from the mess of paperwork on the floor. His face is pale and he looks like he hasn't slept in days.

"I shouldn't be here," he mutters, agitated.

Something starts to shake on the cluttered desk, knocking papers to the floor. It's his cell phone, with an incoming call. JB ignores it.

"I need to be back there with them. This is *stupid*. So stupid."

He flips through some more papers until he finds a yellow form. He angrily stuffs it in a pocket.

His phone vibrates on the desk again as he stands up. He wobbles from the sudden head rush.

When he sets a hand on the empty desk for balance, he hits a silver-framed photo of a brown-haired woman and a little girl of about two. The picture frame falls over with a clatter.

"Damn."

Looking away from the toppled picture, JB finally notices his phone. He grabs it and pauses before answering. His dead-man's stare returns as he touches the silver picture frame.

Then he opens his mouth and starts to inhale before saying hello.

But the word never makes it out of his mouth.

Back in his room at the Home, on the floor with his back to the door, JB sat up abruptly, inhaling loudly. His eyes flashed open and his face turned red.

He did *not* want to remember that day.

"Ah man..."

He crawled slowly over to his bed and dropped onto it with a groan and a loud squeak of the springs.

"I think I need to take the rest of the day off," he muttered to himself in a shaky voice. "I *am* retired, after all."

Reena sat alone at a scratched-up table in the cramped staff room, along with three other chairs, a wallboard covered in patient names, a burnt-smelling coffee pot, and the ancient computer that all the staff had to take turns using.

She tapped in her last note for the day and shut down the computer. The computer let out a few loud shudders and went black.

What a day, she thought. Another one down the drain.

She felt something nagging at the back of her mind, as if she were missing something. She knew from years of experience that she couldn't go home and enjoy what was left of her evening until she'd figured out what was causing that annoying feeling. She looked over the list of names on the wallboard, including one with an ominous black line through it.

She tapped Amelia's name, and scribbled a few words notes after Mr. Stone's name.

"He just can't leave that man alone," she said as she wrote. "Or any of the others. He doesn't belong here..."

She shook her head when she saw matching notes for three patients, each note starting with the words INJURED DURING THERAPY.

Reena's frustration grew as she continued down the list.

There was a special place on the wallboard for "J. Beckwith" down at the bottom. While all the others had therapy sessions and prescriptions next to their names, JB had nothing written by his name except INJURED DURING THERAPY as well.

Reena tapped a finger on the "J" of his name, smudging it.

Good ol' JB, she thought. That was it—the cause of her nagging sensation.

She grabbed her purse and hurried out of the staff room. She started to slam the door behind her, then caught it before the slam woke the residents. Everyone went to bed early here at the Home.

Out in the deserted hall, she walked up to the nurse's desk, where she found nurse LaTanya and nurse aide Megan, a chubby white girl of about nineteen with ear buds in her ears. Both young women jumped at Reena's approach, and they started shuffling papers to look busy.

"Ear buds out, Megan," Reena said in a sharp voice.

Waiting until Megan yanked the buds from her ears, Reena stepped away from the station and stopped at a door with a frosted-glass and a placard stating: WILLARD V. POWELL, WHISPERING PINES ADMINISTRATOR.

Reena cast one last look down the hall, then checked her watch, starting to reconsider her plan of action.

Just as she raised her hand to knock, though, Bart the therapist sidled up to her with an unlit cigar in his mouth.

"D'you hear what happened today in the gym during today's therapy session? Classic JB, I tell ya. Let me buy you dinner and I'll recap."

Reena leaned closer, which made Bart chuckle in surprise. She sniffed and gave him a look.

"You really should wait to start drinking until *after* you leave the property, Bart. That's a firing offense, as I'm sure you know. Put that cigar away, while you're at it."

Bart took a step back, full of bluster now.

"Come on, now," he said. "This place would drive anyone to drink. Even *you.*"

Reena turned from the door and faced Bart, thinking: He's messing with the wrong woman tonight.

"Even me?" she said, fighting to keep her voice low. "It wasn't me who let a patient—client, whatever— take over the therapy room for a game of kickball. *Kickball!* With a room full of elderly! What were you thinking, Bart?"

Bart straightened up and shot a quick glance at LaTanya and Megan rubber-necking this scene. They quickly turned back to their paperwork with more paper-shuffling.

"Okay" he said, defeated. "So, yeah. I really gotta go. Maybe dinner some other night, then?"

Reena just shook her head and stalked off, alone. She pretended not to hear the stifled laughs coming from the nursing station behind her.

She stopped at last at a set of double doors leading to the Alzheimer's unit. It was always quiet in there, as most of the residents there were usually lost somewhere inside their heads. She found peace down here, most days, so long as nobody was having some sort of fit.

She flashed her badge in front of a reader with a beep and pushed open the heavy door.

On the other side of the door, silence immediately enveloped her as she stepped into the subdued lighting of the six-room, carpeted Alzheimer's unit. The rooms were spread out a bit more down here, instead of crowding in on each other like it was in the rest of the Home.

Each door was slightly ajar, and a soft voice came from the last room on the right. Curious, Reena tiptoed toward that room, whispering to herself, "Miss *Wilkerson?*"

MICHAEL JASPER

She peeked into the room, and indeed it was Miss Wilkerson, a white-haired black woman of 91, talking in a deep, melodic voice.

"We'd hang the sheets out to dry by eight a.m. each day and then sneak back inside for cig'rettes an' a shot of somethin' dark in our coffees. Nobody knew what we was up to. And them sheets smelled like heaven when we brung 'em back in. Only took an hour or two to dry in that ungodly Carolina heat. No customer ever complained. Except that time Alisa forgot to wash up after our smoke break. We sure missed her after they fired her."

The woman had a severe tremor in her head and hands, and her brown eyes were lost in both her memories and her cloudy cataracts. But her voice was clear.

Smiling, Reena moved closer and then froze when she heard a soft, but all-too-familiar voice.

"*That* was a firing offense, Miss W?"

It was JB. Down here in the restricted unit. Reena's smile disappeared.

"You'd better believe it, sonny," Miss Wilkerson answered. "The Riverside Inn wa'n't the best place to stay in Durham County for no small reason. They had them some *standards*, y'see."

"I believe it. But *man*. That's harsh."

Reena couldn't believe it. JB had snuck down here, and now he was sitting and chatting with Miss W as if they were lifelong friends. Reena gripped the door frame next to her to keep from screaming at him.

"You didn't question things back then, JB. Not when the bosses was all white."

"Hmm," JB said, a bit awkwardly. "Well." He clears his throat. "Guess that's why you shouldn't smoke, huh?"

Miss W laughed at that, a soft sound like rain.

Reena stepped closer, fighting her nursely urge to break it up to prevent another upset patient like Marvin earlier. But the clarity of Miss Wilkerson's voice stopped her.

"Ain't nothin' gonna hurt you from a few cig'rettes. Them smoke breaks is what kept us workin' through them ten-hour days. We wouldn'a gotten through them long days without my cig'rettes and my lovely, dear friends. It was good work. *Hard* work, but good. Even with the boss man, who was whiter than you, my friend." Miss Wilkerson took a shaky breath. "It made for a good life, JB. A lot of my friends, well, they didn't have it as good as me. I got *lucky.*"

After a few moments of silence, Reena couldn't help herself. She peeked into the room.

JB sat in a chair right next to Miss W's bed, holding her hand and smiling like a saint.

At a loss, Reena just gazed at him. Who *was* this guy?

Then she glanced at Miss W, who had drifted off to sleep with a contented, toothless smile. Miss W began snoring softly.

"Ahem," Rena said.

JB jumped a tiny bit at the interruption, but he was careful not to wake Miss W. He gave Reena a ridiculously enthusiastic thumbs-up as he half jogged, half limped out of the room toward her, eyes blazing.

Reena bit back a smile at his unabashed joy, remembering her frustration with him and his antics from earlier today.

"Did you *see* that?" JB said as they walked slowly back toward the entrance to the wing. "Did you hear that story? Omigod."

Reena wasn't having any of his enthusiasm. Not right now. "Does the concept of 'off-limits' mean anything to you, Mr. Beckwith?"

"I mean, really. That smile on her face? Priceless."

"Mr. Beckwith."

"So awesome. I love it."

"Mr. *Beckwith.*"

JB stopped and turned to her, surprised at her annoyed tone.

"Hmmm?" he said.

They stopped in front of the double doors leading to the rest of the Home.

"I need the badge you must've borrowed to get down here. I'm not going to ask how you got it, or who you got it from. Just hand it over."

With a sheepish grin, JB reached into the pocket of his khaki pants and pulled out a beige badge.

"Ah, man. Really? This thing comes in handy when I—"

"*Yes*, really. You could get this place shut down with this behavior. You broke all sorts of rules coming down here."

JB handed her the badge along with a scowl.

"Seems like a silly bunch of rules," he said, completely without any remorse. "I mean, we were just talking. And she was doing great! She was *right there*! I don't see Bart or anyone else talking to her like that. Or even listening to her, for that matter..."

Reena bristled at that.

"That's none of your business. You're not even a real res— Ah. Never mind."

JB nodded and looked back down the hall toward Miss W's room. His face went blank, just for a moment.

"Fine," he said. "It's my bedtime anyway."

He pushed the door open and limped off without another word.

Reena let the door swing back shut, leaving her in the softly lit, silent Alzheimer's wing.

"That does it, she says as she stuffed the borrowed badge into her pocket. "Powell needs to know about this."

She left the Alzheimer's unit and approached the administrator's door with its frosted glass window. She raised a hand to knock on the door, only to have the door swing open suddenly.

She had time to jump back a few steps to keep Mr. Powell from running her over. He wasn't even looking where he was going, so when he saw Reena standing there, he let out a surprised yelp and dropped his briefcase, spilling its contents onto the hall floor.

"Whoops!" Powell said in a voice tight with stress. "Sorry! I, ah, didn't hear anyone out here."

Powell cleared his throat and bent down to pick up briefcase with its spilled papers and thumb drives. But Reena already had them gathered up for him. She dropped the the papers and the tiny drives back into his briefcase and closed it with a snap.

"Huh," Powell said. "You got it to *close*. Nice."

"Mister Powell," Reena began. "I know it's late, but could we talk? It's about one of the residents. I mean, clients."

Powell glanced at the door next to the nurse station with the red EXIT sign over it, and then nodded reluctantly at Reena.

"Of course," he said in an unconvincing voice. "Clients come first. *Always*."

He held the door open and awkwardly took the briefcase from Reena's hand. Glancing at the nicely framed pictures and degrees on the walls, Reena took a seat on the chair in front of his big brown desk.

Powell settled into his leather chair, holding his briefcase in front of him like a shield. He had a baby-faced look to him, Reena had always thought, though he had to be in his mid to late forties. He'd inherited his position from his father, the *real* Mister Powell, just three years ago. Reena had respected the real Mister Powell.

"So," the young Mister Powell said. "Is everything all right?"

"Most every*one* is all right. But we've had some injuries today. Minor ones, but people have been hurt."

Powell leaned forward as best he could with his briefcase wedged in his lap.

"Injuries? How bad?"

"Minor, like I said," Reena had to force the annoyance from her voice. "A hamstring pull, a twisted ankle. A case of dehydration."

Powell crinkled up his nose. "You know, I don't really involve myself in the medical side of the clients' lives."

"I know. But the *cause* for all three client issues is the same. You see, I heard that at therapy today, Jay—"

Reena stopped in surprise when something buzzed inside her purse. An instant later, when another buzz occurred, she realized with embarrassment that it was her phone. She pulled it out and flipped it open to see the caller ID.

"I'm sorry," she said. "I've got to take this. It's my daughter."

She stood, holding a hand over the phone, and took a few steps away from Powell's desk.

"Stacia? What is it, honey? What's wrong?" Reena listened to Stacia's explanation for a moment. It was the neighbor kid Teddy, harassing her again. "I'm on my way home. I just have to finish up some work stuff."

Reena looked up and threw Powell an apologetic look. He gave her a weak smile and fidgeted with his watch and briefcase.

"I've really got to get going, Reena," he said. "I need to meet someone."

Reena abruptly forgot about Powell, focused only on her call when Stacia mentioned Teddy again.

"*What?*" she said, trying not to shout into the phone in her boss's office. "No. No way. Do *not* let him come in the house, him or anyone else. Do you hear me? Okay. Good. I'll be home in twenty minutes. Love you. Bye now."

She slipped her phone back into her purse as Powell stood up. She was about to apologize, but he cut her off.

"I've got to get to my meeting at 8:30," Powell said. "It's a, uh, business dinner thing. I'm sorry, but can we postpone until tomorrow? I'm really running late."

As Powell carried his briefcase past her to the door, Reena stood fixed in the middle of the room.

"Uh, sure," she said. "*Tomorrow.*"

Powell opened the door and looked at his watch, nearly losing his briefcase and papers all over again.

"Would you mind pulling the door shut behind you? I've got to run."

And with that, he was gone.

Reena remained in the middle of the office, smoldering with anger for a few seconds, hands tapping on her purse.

"Sure. No problem, boss. If we have half the Home in crutches and casts tomorrow, thanks to your special *client,* that is no problem. My staff and I will take care of it. And I'd be happy to pull the door shut for you, too, you slack-ass piece of..."

Reena walked out of Powell's office and slammed the door behind her instead of finishing her sentence. She gave the nurses across the hall a wicked grin.

Hope that didn't wake up too many residents—or should I say *clients*—for you nurses.

She reached into her purse for her keys and turned to the exit. Before pulling her hand out of her purse, though, she paused. She made a detour instead toward the door for the kitchen.

"Just five more minutes," she told herself as she made her way through the darkened kitchen toward the loading dock outside. She propped open the metal door that led from the kitchen to the dirty, grease-stained loading dock, which was poorly lit by a streetlight. A reeking dumpster sat next to the dock.

Shivering from the cold, she pulled a pack of cigarettes from her purse, lit a cigarette, and inhaled the smoke hungrily. She exhaled, looking up at the reddening sunset.

I hate this nasty habit, she thought, as a peaceful look crossed her face. She closed her eyes and took another drag.

As if on cue, JB sauntered out of the kitchen, limping a bit. Reena's eyes flipped open in surprise, which quickly turned to anger.

JB nodded at her, unsurprised by her presence here. He started pacing around the dock, as if working out the kinks in his bad knee, breathing in and out loudly. His breath steamed in the cold.

Her moment of peace ruined, Reena dropped her cigarette to the ground and ground it out.

"Like a bad penny," she muttered.

JB heard her, but he didn't even break stride.

"Hey now. Manners! And those things'll kill you, ya know. Or at least get you into trouble, just like in Miss W's story."

"You shouldn't be *out* here, ya know."

JB shrugged and paced some more around the dock, like an overactive kid who couldn't get to sleep. He tottered a bit on the edge of the dock.

"No worries. I'm just winding down from the day. Trying to keep the old knee from locking up. And what a *day*, huh? Lots of great things happening here today." Still doing his crazy version of pacing, he shot a look over at Reena. "So. How's your daughter Stacey? Junior high agreeing with her?"

"*Stacia* is fine. She just is having issues with a... oh, never mind."

JB gave her an eyebrows-raised look, about to pursue that topic, then he stopped. "Are you really smoking *generic* cigarettes? Do you really hate yourself that much? Brr."

Reena didn't know which rude statement to respond to first. "You—*what*? I... Mr. Beckwith, I don't think that's any of your busi—"

JB held up his hands in front of him. "I'm sorry. I didn't mean it like that. It's just. You shouldn't smoke. You're a nurse and all." He paused, thinking for a moment. "I mean, nursing *director*. You're in the health profession, and here you are smoking cancer sticks. Coffin nails. Wacky tobaccy."

Reena just stared at JB while he talked and paced, wondering when he'd run out of steam. Finally he stopped and looked at her a bit sheepishly. They stared at one another for an awkward couple of moments.

Reena surprised herself by laughing and breaking the tension.

"Did LaTanya give you somebody else's meds by accident?"

"Ha," JB said, "I wish! Nah. I'm just a bit cranked up from the day. Cranked up, and feeling *lucky*."

Reena gave JB a closer look, not expecting this.

"Lucky?"

"Yeah. To get to meet all the folks here and to get to listen to their stories. It's amazing. *You* know how it is. You see them every day. *You're* lucky."

Reena rubbed her mouth, thinking about that. It was as if he'd found something that had been missing in her job for years. Something that he had uncovered almost effortlessly in his short time here.

"Well, *yeah*," she said, as if this was all obvious to her, too. "Of course."

"I think," JB said, almost to himself, "that's why I'm here."

Reena stepped closer, crushing the pack of smokes in her hand. "What'd you say?"

"Oh," JB said. "Nothing. Just blabbering. That's what I do, you know?"

He crossed his arms over his chest and took a couple long strides to the door, working his knee again.

"It's late," he said. "Gotta get some sleep. Big day tomorrow. *Big* day! Brr. And it's supposed to be nice and warm, too. *Finally*."

Reena was still playing one word around in her head: *lucky.*

JB moved closer. "You saw how great Miss Wilkerson is doing, right? It's amazing. Just talking. Sitting there, talking and listening. It's therapeutic, ya know?"

"Yeah, but," Reena began, then changed tactics. "Look, you need to stop this reckless behavior with the residents. You know, the people who *belong* here? These old folks are going to get hurt."

"Yeah, yeah. But the *memories* they'll have!" As he spoke, his voice grew louder. "They won't have to look way back at the distant past for good memories. They'll have them right here and now. In the *present!* Maybe even Miss Amelia will wake up. And who knows what sort of stories she'll tell? I can't wait—"

Reena put a hand on his arm, which was tight and almost quivering with energy.

"Shhh. Take it easy," she said. She took her hand off JB's arm. "So you think that's your *job* here? Your purpose? To show these poor, sick, dying people a good *time*?"

JB shrugged and did some more stretches, obviously uncomfortable talking about himself. "Well yeah. Like I said. Maybe that's why I'm here."

Reena gazed up at the street light again. "Funny," she said in a soft voice. "I've been here almost six years myself. And I still don't know why *I'm* here.

"What do you mean?"

They looked at each other for a long moment. Finally Reena just shrugged, refusing to answer him.

Getting the drift, JB moved toward the door to the kitchen, still limping a bit.

Reena looked down at the damage she'd done to her pack of cigarettes. She walked across the dock and tossed the whole works into the dumpster.

When she turned back to talk to JB again, he was gone.

"Okay," Reena said, walking inside and kicking the door shut behind her. "Be that way."

Hunkered down in the shadows between a shed and chain link fence, JB looked back at the loading dock in shock when he heard the door to the kitchen click shut.

"Crap!" he whispered to himself. "Did she just lock me out?"

Then he remembered why he was out there: Peterson's errand. He looked behind him at a darkened spot in the chain link fence. He'd seen movement out there earlier, but he hadn't said a word about that to Reena.

"Guys?" he called out softly. "Hey, guys. Peterson sent me. It's okay. All clear!"

He waited a moment, listening. Then he lowered himself to the weeds around the shed and fence and rested his head on his knees in the cold.

"Should've known better than to go rogue, just to help out the janitor. Brr."

After another self-pitying moment, JB got up and brushed himself off. He started walking toward the narrow driveway between the Home and the chain-link fence, watching his shadow grow bigger from the spotlight behind him.

He made it about twenty feet down the road before he looked to the left and nearly fell over in shock.

Two people stood on the other side of the fence, dressed in black hoodies, staring at him in silence. JB couldn't tell if they were old or young, male or female.

"Holy friggin' crap. You two scared the life outta me. My heart."

The taller person in black let out a derisive laugh from under his or her hoodie. "Told you that wasn't him. This dude's *white*, man."

"Don't get no whiter than him," the second person said. "He 'bout glows in the dark."

Both of them laughed, and that was when JB deduced that they were female, probably in their late teens. He pulled himself together and eyed both strangers.

"All right, you're black, I'm white. Now that we got that established, you want to tell me if you know Peterson or not? 'Cause he's white, too. Just like me. And he had an errand for me."

"When'd *you* start working here, chunky monkey?" the first girl asked.

"Don't give me a hard time about my weight. The food here is carb-heavy. It's not my fault." JB realized how lame that sounded and felt his face grow hot. "And I don't work here. I'm a resident."

The girls broke up into laughter again.

"We must be at the wrong place, then," the first girl said. "We're lookin' for an old-folks home, not some fat-white-folks home."

JB took a few steps closer to the girls, annoyed.

"What'd I say about the weight cracks? You two need to go home."

The second girl stepped closer to the fence as well, no longer joking. "What you doin' out here, man, with no coat on or nothing? You lookin' to score some weed? That what that Peterson guy sent you here for?"

"He's off tonight," JB said. He couldn't believe he was even having this conversation. "I told him I'd keep an eye out for him. But he didn't say anything about two ladies like you hooking him up."

"Did he really just say 'hooking'?" the first girl said with a laugh. "Oh God, Manda. This is better than what we were sent here to do. Way better."

"All right," JB said, heading back up the gravel drive toward the street. "It's a free country. Stay there if you want to. I'm going back inside."

As he stomped down the dark road toward the front entrance, the two girls crunched through the weeds on the other side of the fence, wordlessly keeping pace with him.

"Nothing good on TV tonight?" JB called out.

The girls both made annoying TSK-ing sounds and kept walking along with him.

"This is doing nothing for my perception of the quality of this neighborhood, you know."

The girls reached the end of the chain-link fence and stepped onto the sidewalk shared by the empty lot and the Home. With one last glance in their direction, JB scurried toward the front entrance and tried the door. Locked.

The two girls cracked up from their spot on the sidewalk. JB softly knocked on the door.

"*Megan*!" he whispered as loudly as he dared. "Take out your stupid ear buds!"

A few long moments passed, but nobody answered his knocks. The girls whispered together, and then they TSKed at him again.

"Have a good night on the street, man!" the first girl called out. "Stay warm."

"And tell Willard," added the girl with the meaner voice, "that Rubin's peeps said hey, and that we missed 'im tonight!"

JB gave them a go-on gesture and sank back against the door, much like he did in his room earlier.

"Youth is wasted on the young," he muttered. "Especially the young and the mean."

He sat rubbing his arms as the sounds of the girls' voices and footsteps faded. The chirping of crickets and frogs grew louder.

His eyes closed, and he was about to nod off, but then the door to the Home was yanked open by Megan, and JB rolled backwards into safety once more.

Reena finally made it back to her small, tidy apartment. When she dropped her purse and her bag of books onto the kitchen counter, an Anatomy textbook slid free of her bag, nearly fell to the floor, but Reena managed to snag it.

Before she could slip the textbook back into the bag, her twelve-year-old daughter Stacia stepped up behind her, sniffing her.

"*Cigarettes*, Mom," she said. "I smell 'em on you!"

"There you are, girl," Reena said. "I was starting to wonder if you'd taken off or something. Didn't you hear me come in?"

"Don't change the subject. You've been smoking again. I wish I could ground *you*."

Reena turned and gave her daughter a calculating look, trying to decide whether to confirm or deny the accusations. She opted for honesty. "I just had one..."

Stacia threw her hands in the air in frustration and dropped into a chair at their kitchen table, which was covered with Stacia's homework.

"Mo-o-om!" she said, laying on the guilt. "So *that*'s why you were so late. Taking an extra-long smoke break while Teddy the Terrorizer from next door was *stalking* me."

Reena sat down next to her and pulled her chair close, her shame about sneaking cigarettes gone in an instant.

"I'm gonna have to talk to that boy's mother. This makes me so damn *mad*—"

"Well, maybe *stalking* is too strong a word," Stacia said as she inched her chair back from Reena. "Teddy only called me twice. And he keeps on texting me. Says he wants to come over and..." She made air quotes and deepened her voice: "spend some quality time with you. So long as your mom ain't home, that is."

Reena shook her head, furious again for what felt like the hundredth time today.

"I'm so *tired* of people ignoring boundaries. And thinking the world is theirs to do with it whatever they please. Harassing people all the time—"

Stacia patted Reena's hand, stopping her in mid-rant.

"Mom. He's just a harmless boy. It's okay. I can handle him." She tried to laugh it off. "Just... chill out, okay? You're sort of foaming at the mouth."

Reena touched her mouth, as if checking for spittle. Then she gave Stacia a "busted" look. They both started laughing.

"You're right," Reena said. "I just hate having you home by yourself at night. I wish some days I had a normal job that didn't require twelve-hour shifts."

"*Mom.* You know doctors work insane hours too. You sure you want to keep taking those classes?"

"A physician assistant is a lot different from a doctor. I won't have hours like that. I just wish I didn't need so many credits to graduate."

Stacia began pushing her homework into a neat stack. "No worries. We'll study together, then. Here. I'll make some room."

Reena rubbed her daughter's back and smiled. Then she got up to grab her bag of books and bring them to the table.

She took a good, long look at the books, papers, and folders already spread out over most of the table. "Stacia. How much homework are they *giving* you? Are you in seventh grade or grad school?"

"Eh, it's mostly busy work. But yeah, my English teacher is *killing* us. Making us read *The Iliad* and crap."

"Wow. That's kinda heavy for twelve-year-olds."

"Tell me 'bout it. Terry went through his copy of the book and highlighted all the gory parts."

Reena just shook her head. For a few minutes they got busy with their homework, writing on notebooks and paging through textbooks.

Stacia sniffed again and peeked over at her mom. She waggled a warning finger at her. "Don't think that I'm forgetting about the cigarettes, missy."

"I smoked my last one tonight. I just had a crazy-stressful day today, that's all."

"Good. I mean, not good that you had a bad day. But good that you're not giving yourself cancer no more."

"*Any* more," Reena said, automatically shifting into Mother mode.

Stacia made a face and then flipped through a battered English textbook. "Did you know that this Iliad is one long poem? A two-hundred-page poem, Mom! You should feel *lucky* not to have to read all this." Stacia sighs. "Homer was a dork."

Reena let out a distracted laugh. Thinking about something Stacia said, she gazed out the kitchen window, thinking.

"Yeah," she said at last. "I'm lucky. That's me. Feeling *lucky*." She looked over at her daughter, engrossed in the details of the Trojan War.

Maybe it wasn't such a bad day after all, she thought, if I got to end it like this, with my girl.

She nodded, as if making a decision. She closed her Anatomy book with a pop and grabbed Stacia's arm.

"Hey," Reena said. "Do we have any of those cookies left? Let's grab 'em and see what's on the tube. All these books can wait 'til tomorrow. Homer the dork can wait."

"Mom! You're crazy!"

Stacia tried to fight her off, but Reena pried the textbook out of her grip. Stacia broke out laughing.

Reena rushed off with the book into the kitchen, laughing too.

"Not crazy," she said. "Not me. Not one bit..."

* * * * *

JB stands in an intensive-care hospital room, immersed in an unnatural silence.

His face is desperate, hopeless, and he's too drained to even speak.

He's standing next to a bed. Intensive-care equipment surrounds him and the bed, but there's no beeping sounds. Just surreal silence. Snow falls on the other side of the small window.

He has the yellow form he found back in his home office stuffed into his back pocket.

He looks like he's holding someone's hand in both of his, gripping it like a lifeline as tears fill his eyes. But the bed's empty.

JB stands there, lips moving, but no sound comes out.

The dead look fills his eyes as a pair of tears slip down his cheeks.

He moves closer to the empty bed, closer, and closer, until he's falling face-first into it.

The world turns white for a beat...

...Then JB is lying face-first in a different bed.

When he gets up from the bed, the room has changed into his small, sparse room at Whispering Pines Rest Home.

He's still wearing the same clothes, though. And he has the yellow paper in his hand. It reads: PROOF OF HEALTH INSURANCE.

All alone in the room, JB circles and bangs against the walls, but can't make a sound. He can't find the door.

He drops the yellow paper and tries to yell, but can't make a sound.

Just... Silence.

JB panics.

He can't find the door, and he can't get out.

Face-down in his bed, JB woke with a start, sucking in a sudden breath. He rolled onto his back, eyes wide, covered in sweat.

"No," he murmured. It was the dream again. "No no no..."

He sat up and spied the door leading into the hall. He exhaled with relief, glad there's a way out, unlike his dream.

With a supreme effort, he forced the terror of his nightmare from his face and him mind, turning the fear to enthusiasm when he remembered what day it was today.

"*Yes.* Today's the big day. Our field trip! They're gonna love it."

He rushed to the bathroom, splashed water on his face, and headed for the door, already thinking through his plans and the adventures they would have today.

He threw a glance at the desk before touching the doorknob.

"You guys would've loved this place, too," he whispered.

And then he crept out into the hall, silent as a shadow.

JB softly knocked twice on three different doors, seemingly at random. Each door opened a heartbeat after his knock, and a smiling, excited, elderly face poked out. JB grinned down the hall as Nelly, Marvin, and Abe emerged from their rooms. Nelly and Marvin grinned back, and grumpy old Abe gave his best approximation of a smile, which on his dark brown face looked a lot like a frown.

JB motioned for them all to follow him, and they tiptoed and rolled down the hall. They stopped in front of a battered door with a red Emergency Exit sign affixed to it.

JB held a single finger up to his mouth for silence, and then he ever-so-gently opened the door. His three partners-in-crime winced, and then they all exhaled when the alarm failed to go off.

"Let's roll," JB said as helped them all out the door. He couldn't stop smiling.

They walked out the door, Abe bringing up the rear in painfully slow fashion, his walker squeaking and scraping against the sidewalk with every other step the old man took.

The four of them walked down the weedy, trash-dotted sidewalk of this not-so-great part of town, JB in the lead for half a block or so. Then he hurried back to speed Abe along. And then JB jumped ahead to scope things out at the head of the pack.

They continued this back-and-forth process down about three blocks, past a few closed-down business and boarded-up houses. They passed a black man and woman sitting on their front porch, and JB waved at them in what he hoped was a confident enough manner to prevent a trio of Silver Alerts from being reported.

Slightly out of breath, Nelly looked over at Marvin. "Why in the world did JB ask *him*?" She nodded back at Abe, who JB was trying to goad into a slightly faster pace, without much luck.

Marvin shook his head and breathed in deeply of the morning air. "JB can't help himself. He's got to share the love."

Nelly shook her head as JB jogged past them to check out the next block. "That Abe feller never knew a thing about *love*. Always complaining about everything."

"But Abe wanted to go. JB couldn't tell them man no," Marvin said, and then he pointed at a fence ahead of them. "Hush now. We're almost there."

At last, with JB working up a sweat in the cool late-winter air, they arrived at their destination: The Enlightened Child Daycare Center. The "C" on the center's front sign dangled crookedly as a loose tooth.

JB gave his three fellow residents a triumphant smile as he held the gate open for them to enter the playground. "After you, fellow adventurers!"

At the Enlightened Child, the playground equipment was old, the toys were faded, and the weeds were choking out the sandbox, but the daycare was still a joyful place full of happy kids. The kids' winter coats were all off, littering the playground in deference to the warm breezes of spring.

In just a few minutes, JB and his three fellow residents were busy playing with the kids—most of whom were black, and *all* of whom were incredibly cute.

JB started off at the swings, pushing kids, and then taking a turn on a swing himself. After a few big kicks, he leapt off the swing into the air, his round face red with laughter as he floated through the air for a few wonderfully weightless seconds.

Nelly climbed the slide, arms shaking as she reached to the top. She paused for a heart-stopping moment to look around, suddenly apprehensive. The she threw caution to the wind and slid down, laughing.

Marvin was busy building in the weedy sandbox, creating a huge, multi-sided castle while happily directing a half dozen kids in his construction endeavors.

Meanwhile, Abe sat on a playground bench as kids climbed all over him and his walker as if they were both new pieces of playground equipment. He looked miserable, but every now and then he let a smile slip out.

The three women working at the daycare nodded and waved at JB, glad to have a break from their duties for this repeat visit by JB and his elderly friends.

Reena coasted into the office, a smile on her face and a bounce in her step. She felt like she'd found a new outlook on life after stopping everything to spend time with Stacia and think about where her life was going right now.

Unfortunately, it was an outlook that lasted just a few seconds longer. It all went sour when she saw the look on LaTanya's stressed-face at the nurse station.

"What is it?" Reena asked her.

LaTanya jumped, and then shook her head. "We have three wanderers."

Reena dropped her coat. "*Damn* it. Who? How long?"

"I found out about it right before you walked in. It's Mr. Marvin, Ms. Nelly, and Abe."

Reena would've laughed if she hadn't been so mad.

"Abe?" she asked. "And his *walker*?"

LaTanya licked her lips nervously. She took a nervous breath. "And JB's gone, too," she whispered.

"Of course," Reena said.

She pushed off from LaTanya's desk and marched down the hall towards the residents' rooms. Her mind was going a mile a minute, thinking of all the bad things that could happen to her old folks. She turned to call back to LaTanya, then she lowered her voice and stepped closer to her fellow nurse.

"Call 911 and tell them—wait, no. Not yet. Get Bart up here now. And Peterson, too, if he's not too baked already."

"Right. I just saw Peterson in the kitchen, looking for snacks."

"Go," Reena said, and the two women rushed off in opposite directions.

Reena headed right to JB's room and yanked open the door, her good mood from last night completely gone. As she'd expected, the room was empty. But she hadn't expected the room to be so Spartan, without a hint that a human actually lived there other than the unmade bed.

"Where'd you take them, Mr. Beckwith?" she whispered, as if his deserted room could answer. "You didn't just up and *leave*, did you?"

But when she checked the closet, his shoes and clothes were all hanging there, mostly khaki pants and golf shirts. Therapist attire.

She gave the room another once-over, shaking her head.

So *empty*, she thought, taken aback by the way JB had been living. Then she remembered the three missing residents and hurried back into the hall. She'd deal with JB's issues later.

She knocked on Marvin's door, then Nelly's, then Abe's. No luck at any of rooms. They were all gone.

"Out giving them some new *memories*, I'll bet," she muttered on her way back to the nurse station. She paused to peer through the frosted glass of Powell's office. She could just make out the outline of two people sitting in Powell's chair. She paused, about to knock, and then she thought twice about interrupting.

This needn't concern him, anyway, she thought. Not yet.

She was on her way back when Bart appeared, his eyes bloodshot, and his shirt littered with bits of donut frosting.

"Hey, hey. Slow down, Reena. We'll find them." He noticed the frosting on his shirt and started brushing at it. "How far could they have gotten?"

"Nobody's in the gym?" she asked him, ignoring his question.

Bart shook his head. "No clients yet today. They're all sleepin' in, far as I can tell."

Reena glared at Bart, unable to stop herself from lashing out at him. "Far as you can tell with your *hangover*, huh?"

Bart pulled away from her, stung. He spluttered but couldn't come up with a good comeback.

Truth hurts, Reena thought as she walked past him, headed for the nurse station again.

LaTanya stood there with Peterson the janitor, who looked as disheveled and tired as Bart.

LaTanya was furious. "They left through the emergency exit down the hall," she said. "The emergency buzzer's *busted*. Has been for almost two damn weeks."

"You're kidding. How did—"

LaTanya pointed at Peterson, who cleared his throat. "Mister Powell said to just keep it *locked* 'til we had the funds to fix it."

"*Great*," Reena said. "Too late to do anything about that. LaTanya, stay here and keep your cell phone handy. I'll call if I need you." She pointed at Peterson and Bart. "You two are coming with me."

Without a word of complaint, the two men followed Reena at a safe distance as she strode down the hall toward the side door that JB had used earlier. Reena tried not to panic as she thought of the hundreds of places their missing residents might be. The city was small, but spread out. They could be *anywhere*.

Reena went out the side door, followed by Bart and Peterson. She pushed away her rising wave of fear, knowing that her emotions would just make everything that much worse. She had to stay in control.

"Come on," she told the other two members of her posse. "Let's go."

Back at the playground, Marvin was still in the middle of the big sandbox, talking and laughing with his group of young boys who hung on his every word. Meanwhile Nelly was monitoring the line of kids at the slide, and the kids were all orderly and patient. When addressed, they said "yes, ma'am" or "no ma'am" to her. Even Abe had found a new friend or two to regale him with stories about lunch or dolls or trains.

Over by the swings, JB had just finished up moderating an argument between two boys about a truck. The boys wiped their tears away and then shook hands like adults. Situation defused.

As the boys walked off peacefully, JB pumped his fist in victory. This day was shaping up to be better than he'd ever hoped.

Over in the sandbox, Marvin and the boys had finished up their sand castle construction. The boys laughed along with something Marvin just said.

Then the old man paused for a moment, and his eyes clouded over. He stopped laughing.

From halfway across the playground, JB caught the change in Marvin. He started walking toward the sandbox as fast as he could.

A heartbeat later, Marvin was standing up straight inside the sandbox, frowning.

"Hey!" JB shouted, trying to get his elderly friend's attention. "Marvin! Hey buddy!"

But the old man didn't seem to have any idea where he was right now. In his confusion, he stepped on the sand castle he and his little friends had been working on all morning. Kids cried out in fear and ran away from him.

JB reached Marvin's side just as Reena, Bart, and Peterson walked through the gate to the playground.

"Marvin," JB said. "Mr. Stone. It's okay."

"What are you *talking* about?" Marvin said. "And why are we in a playground?

"It's all right, Mr. Stone," JB said, doing his best impression of a therapist or a nurse from the Home. "It was just a little break in the day. A quick trip outside."

Marvin had his chin up, like he was spoiling for a fight with JB. "Don't talk to me like I'm five," he said.

JB stepped back, only to have Bart the therapist show up out of nowhere.

Bart grabbed Marvin by the upper arm, and Marvin reacted by swinging and punching Bart right on the chin. They both went down. The few remaining kids near the sandbox freaked out and ran.

JB dove into the fray, trying to separate the two men. Bart was fighting and kicking, but Marvin had him in a sleeper hold. Nelly rushed over, holding the hands of two little girls, while Abe started the long, slow walk across the playground toward the sandbox slash wrestling ring.

Reena and the three black women who worked at the day care rushed over as well, leaving a stunned, slightly stoned Peterson with the kids.

"This is so awesome, isn't it, little guys?" Peterson cackled to the kids all around him. "Kick his butt, Marvin!"

Reena got right in Marvin's face. "Mr. Stone," she cried. "Let go of him! It's Bart. Your friend from the Home! Mr. Stone!"

With a grunt, Marvin released Bart. The younger man dropped down onto the sand face-first, knocked unconscious by Marvin's wrestling hold.

Marvin turned on Reena, but pointed at JB. "This *white* boy keeps trying to tell me that everything's all right. This white boy."

"Hey," JB began, but Reena stepped between him and Marvin.

"*Stop*," she said to JB. "Haven't you done enough damage today? Just *step away* so we can get everyone back where they belong. Okay?"

JB nodded and brushed sand off his pants, unable to look at Marvin's face.

"Hmmph," Marvin said, still glowering at JB. "No white man has ever been the boss of me. *Never.*"

Still down in the sand, Bart woke abruptly and rolled into a sitting position. "What *happened*?" he said groggily. "Did someone hit me?"

JB stepped back, disappointment and guilt on his red face. "Sorry, Marvin," he murmured. "Sorry, kids."

A tiny elbow hit JB in the knee, and he winced—it was his bad knee. He looked down and saw a little black girl of about four, looking up at him.

"Why you sorry?" she asked him. "Did *you* make the old man get mad?"

JB hunkered down, with a good bit of pain in his knee, until he was at eye level with the girl.

"It wasn't *officially* my fault. But I think I sort of helped make him mad. When people get old, sometimes they... well, it's hard to explain."

The little girl nodded sagely. "They get a little cuckoo. My great-gram got that way. She was always singing old songs and calling me the wrong name."

As Reena and the staffers from the Home and the daycare got everyone up and calm, JB laughed softly with the little girl.

"You're smart," he said. "That's exactly right. I'm JB. What's your name?"

"Halle. Like the actress. But my hair's longer than hers."

"Nice to meet you, Halle. Your hair is way better than any actress's hair I've ever seen."

Halle peered at him closely, her tiny eyebrows lowered. "Are *you* a little cuckoo, too?"

The question caught JB off-guard. He blinked at her for a few seconds, trying to find an answer. His smile turned to a look of intense sadness. Sadness and loss. This little girl was so close to her age...

Then JB regained control of his emotions. He forced a laugh and shook his head at Halle.

"Nope," he said. "Not cuckoo. Just a bit crazy, that's all."

When JB stood up straight again, he realized that Reena was just a few feet away, watching him and Halle intently. Her face had softened a bit from the hard and angry mask she'd been wearing just a few minutes earlier.

"JB?" Reena said. "I mean, Mr. Beckwith? We've got to go."

JB reached down for a high five with his little friend. "Nice to meet you, Halle. You take care of yourself, okay?"

"Okay," Halle said as he walked off, limping slightly. "Will do."

Fifteen very chaotic minutes later, Reena had made sure that Nelly, Marvin, and Abe were safely back in their rooms, uninjured and properly hydrated. She had even had the presence of mind to thank Bart and Peterson for their help, something she often forgot to do in moments of crisis like today.

That only left one last thing to do. Deal with JB.

With Bart once more at her side, she knocked on JB's door.

"It's open," JB called in a tired voice.

When they went inside, JB was sitting on his unmade bed, staring at the closed blinds of his window. Reena took a seat on his desk chair, while Bart stood behind her, as if blocking JB from the door to the hall to prevent another escape.

"So," Reena began in a calm, quiet voice. "We had quite the situation this morning, Mr. Beckwith."

"I know. Just lemme explain—"

Reena's voice went even softer.

"*No*. Let me do the explaining right now," she said. "We got there just in time this morning. Do you know that Mr. Stone has a history of violence, most of it as a result of his early-onset dementia? But some of it occurred before he ever came here. I don't suppose the two of you have chatted about *that* during one of your many conversations, have you?"

JB opened his mouth to answer her, and then he simply shook his head, no.

"Or that Miss Nelly is on a combination of medicines for her heart condition? That she's not supposed to exert herself too much? Which would kind of rule out kickball games and slides at the playground, I'd say. Were you aware of that?"

JB's face had turned gray. He shook his head, no, again.

"Or that Abe is... well, he's *95 years old*."

"I *did* know that!" JB blurted out, grasping at straws.

Bart took a step closer to JB, and JB clapped a hand over his own mouth.

"Now, this is all off the record," Reena continued. "Mister Powell wasn't here to witness any of this. And he doesn't need to *know* about the events of this morning."

"I completely agree. Thank—"

"Let me finish."

"Sorry! I just..."

"I'm sharing this confidential information with you because that's just the situation of *three* of your fellow clien—um, residents. I know you're close to nearly everyone in this place. I can give you the delicate medical history of each of them." Reena took a quick breath, trying to keep her anger in check as she thought of all the issues that had arisen since JB's arrival. "They don't *need* someone like you coming in here to get them all worked up. Someone who wants to pretend that they aren't *old*. That they're *not* on the verge of death almost every day. JB. These people are fragile as china. And you're the bull in their china shop.

JB's eyes widened in shock and disbelief. He couldn't believe she was saying all this to him. He was speechless.

"And that's why we need your cooperation," Reena concluded. "We *require* it. And that's why we need you to stay in your room today while we sort things out."

JB sat up straight at that. "But," he began.

He stopped, however, when Bart took another threatening step toward him. JB swallowed, and then he regained his composure. He grinned up at Bart.

"How's the neck, Bart? Mr. Stone still's got it in him, huh?"

Bart stepped back, shoulders slumping, as if tired of playing the bad cop. He let out a reluctant chuckle. "You never give in, do you, JB?"

"*Never*," JB said, still grinning.

"All right, boys," Reena said, getting from the chair and sliding it back into place under the desk. "Are we in agreement with the plan for today?"

"I guess," JB said. "I'm not sure how *legal* this is, but..."

"*No*. Don't talk to me about legal, Mr. Beckwith. Not after this morning. Not after the past six months of you living here in this nursing home. At your age."

JB nodded, without a word.

At the door, Bart waved a hand around the room. "Take care, J-man," he called. "Y'know, you really ought to get some books and some pictures in here. Decorate the place. Make it feel like home."

Reena headed for the door after Bart, and then paused when he stepped away.

"That little girl at the playground," she said, turning back to JB. "You were very sweet to her."

JB felt suddenly cornered, and as Reena talked his sense of being trapped grew.

"I know about your, um. Your history," Reena said, her voice soft, but not harsh like it had been earlier. "You've got to have other family and friends out there who want to see you. But you never have visitors. It's not healthy. And then you take these risks with the elderly people here..."

JB crossed his arms tight over his chest. He couldn't talk about his family or history here. Not right now. Not with her, not with anyone.

"I'd like you to go now," he said.

"I want *everyone* here to be healthy and safe," Reena said. "That includes you, JB."

JB just shook his head, too upset to speak.

"They would've been about the same age, right? Halle and—"

JB jumped to his feet, furious at what felt like a total invasion of his privacy and his past.

Reena moved quickly away from him, fumbling with door in her surprise at JB's reaction. "Okay," she said. "I... I'm sorry. I was just... trying to..."

Reena backed out of the door into the hall, where Bart was waiting with a fat set of keys in his hand.

Standing in the middle of his room, JB just stared at the door as it closed with a bump, and then he heard a jingle of keys and a click. Bart had just locked him in.

JB's legs wobbled as all the tension went out of him. He rested a hand on his desk, as if about to fall over.

Touching the desk brought him back to reality. He reached for the middle desk drawer and started to pull it open.

Then, remembering all that Reena had just told him, he slammed it shut.

JB sits in a chair on the other side of Mr. Powell's big brown desk. He's wearing a slightly dirty blue shirt, and he hasn't showered in a while.

Powell hunches in front of a spread of papers, shaking his head in disbelief. "I'm afraid I've never heard of this sort of thing before, Mr. Beckwith."

JB's face is almost expressionless, except for the haunted look in his eyes. He says nothing, waiting for Powell to continue.

Powell glances up at JB, then looks back at the papers as he talks. What follows sounds like a speech he's given before.

"We specialize in assisted living for the elderly here at Whispering Pines. We have a fine staff of nurses and therapists who are trained in the care of people of *retirement* age. And beyond."

Powell looks up and taps the papers.

"I'm afraid they wouldn't know what to do with you, here, Mr. Beckwith. And, if I might ask, I'm not sure why you would *want* to be here, in a place like this, at your age. You're what—" He glances at a yellow piece of paper. "Thirty-six years old. You've got your whole life ahead of you. You don't really want to be here."

When JB doesn't respond, Powell fidgets and messes with the paper in his hand. "Go live your life. We'll be waiting for you in three or four decades."

JB remains unmoved. He slowly pulls a checkbook from inside his jacket.

"How much?" he asks in a husky voice.

JB has Powell's attention now. Powell's eyes widen. "What do you mean?"

"I've been to five other places around the county. I'm tired of looking. How much do you need to let me live here?"

"You can't be serious. That's not how things *work* here, sir."

"I just got paid a lot of money. A horrible amount of money. So... Would ten thousand dollars a month cover my expenses here?"

Powell mulls this over as he tries to organize JB's papers into a neat stack. He ends up making a bigger mess with his suddenly shaky hands. Finally he looks at JB again.

"Make it twelve a month, six months paid upfront, and we have a deal."

JB nods and starts scribbling out a check.

* * * * *

In his darkened room—lights off, blinds drawn—JB woke in his wooden chair, head down on the desk in front of him.

He rubbed his face and reached out for the small picture in its silver frame. In the weak light of his room, he touched each face frozen in time under the glass, his mind a complete blank other than a dull ache somewhere deep inside his skull. Then he opened the middle drawer and slid the frame back inside it.

A moment later, someone knocked on his door.

"I'd answer," he said, yawning and then wincing at the sudden pins and needles in his legs, "but the door's locked. Remember?"

A jingle of keys sounded from the hallway. JB made sure the middle drawer to his desk was closed before he stumbled over to his bed. He sprawled out, rubbing his sleeping legs.

"Almost forgot I had these," Reena said through the door. "Bart left them with me before he took off for the day."

She unlocked the door and stepped inside. Her face was hidden in shadow from the lights in the hall.

"I just wanted to let you know..." she began, then paused. "Can I come in?

JB clicked on the lamp next to him and covered his head with his pillow to protect his eyes from the brightness. He didn't want to deal with her right now, but he didn't appear to have much choice.

"Sure. C'mon in."

Reena stepped in cautiously. She left the door partially open and stood next to JB's desk.

"I wanted to let you know that everyone's doing fine now. Mr. Stone is calm and getting some good sleep, and Nelly and Abe didn't come away from today's adventure with anything more than a scrape or two. Maybe a new dent on Abe's walker. Those kids loved climbing on that."

"Great," JB said, his voice muffled by the pillow. "No, really. I mean it. I'm glad."

Reena cleared her throat. "Could you maybe put that pillow down? I'd like to talk, just for a minute, before I have to leave for the day."

JB reluctantly set the pillow aside.

"I also wanted to apologize," Reena said. "Bart and I overreacted today. We never should've locked your door. The good thing is that Mr. Powell is totally out of the loop about this morning's incident."

"Good. That's good," JB said.

Reena leaned back on JB's desk, and for a bad moment he thought she was going to try to open the middle drawer.

"You know," she said in a thoughtful, almost distracted voice, "I really liked what you said yesterday, out on the loading dock. How you said you felt *lucky* to be here. I've been thinking about that all day, and even some last night. How this place has felt like a job to me lately, probably because we've had to let two of our nurses go in the past few months, and how we're always busy now. And then on top of that, I'm taking classes in my oh-so-plentiful free time."

JB leaned forward, unable to help himself. He loved a good story.

"In any case," Reena continued, "I'd *lost* that good feeling. Even Nelly said what a great day she had out there today, how it made her miss her grandkids a bit less. Her son and daughter never come to visit. It was nice to sit and talk with her—like *you* would do—instead of rushing off to my next patient. My next *person*. So thanks for the reminder, JB."

JB's long afternoon of solitary confinement was forgotten. He was caught up in Reena's story.

"You're going back to school?" JB said. "I never knew that. What are you studying?"

Reena leaned back the tiniest bit, as if hesitant to talk any more about herself. "Oh, it's this crazy idea I had of becoming a PA. Physician assistant. I'm almost done with all my prerequisite classes. It's taken me forever, too."

"Awesome. You can totally do it. I bet you and Stacia study together all the time."

Reena laughed. "Usually. Sometimes I'm a bad influence on her, though. I distract her."

"Hey, what are moms for?"

Reena smiled at that. She and JB shared a long, wordless look, as if they were finally starting to understand one another.

JB felt an urge to be the first to break the silence. "So yeah," he said. "I really appreciate you stopping by and talking to me. And for unlocking my door, too."

Reena stood and put her hands on her hips, back in nurse mode. "I still stand by what I said earlier, though. Don't push these old folks too hard. It's fine to chat with them. Just *chat*. But their mountain-climbing, bike-riding, extreme-sports days are behind them. Got it?"

JB stood as well, trying unsuccessfully to brush the wrinkles out of his clothes. "Got it."

Reena glanced around the empty room. "Are you sure there isn't someone you'd like to see? We could set up a visit. An old friend? A relative?"

JB shrugged off the question. "All my friends are here. This place is my life now. My new life. Life 2.0."

"Okay. But if you ever need anything—"

"—I'll let you know. Definitely."

They nodded at each other, and JB lifted a hand up halfway, as if to shake with her or to possibly go for a hug. Then he stopped, and his face turned red as he dropped his hand.

Reena tactfully averted her gaze. "Great," she said. "I'd better go."

"Yep," JB nodded. "Thanks again. Just remember what you said about feeling lucky. That's a really good thought."

Reena stepped back abruptly and walked out the door without another word.

It closed with a soft bump, then silence. She left it unlocked. JB was a free man again.

But instead of leaving, he paced slowly around his room, rubbing his chin and trying to figure out Reena. He almost felt sad that she was gone. She'd actually been nice, and compassionate.

Finally, after pacing some more, he snapped his fingers, inspired.

"*Yes*. That's it," he declared. "We are totally going swimming tomorrow."

The next morning, Reena and Stacia sat in front of Stacia's middle school in their car, the motor running to keep the heat going. Reena felt like banging her head against the steering wheel while Stacia dabbed at her eyes. A bell rang from inside the school.

"That's the first bell, Stacia said with a sniff. "I should go."

Reena grabbed her daughter's arm, gently but firmly. "Wait. Is he in one of your morning classes?"

"All of them, and then lunch, too."

Reena glanced at the time on her watch. "Let me go in and talk to the principal, at least."

"No, Mom! That's not why I told you about him. He's just being a pain, that's all."

"I saw what he wrote on your Facebook page. That boy needs a detention. Probably a suspension. I'm so sick of people getting *away* with this sort of thing..."

"Mo-o-om! I'm gonna be late."

Reena sighed. "You and me both. Crap."

Stacia put a hand on Reena's arm. "Mom. I didn't show that to you to get you upset. I just wanted to know what you thought. If you thought Teddy liked me, maybe?"

"That's a messed-up way of showing it! He wrote some ugly stuff..."

Reena saw the worried look on her daughter's face and stopped. Took a breath.

"Okay," she said. "You'd better run. Just let me know if he ever says that stuff to you to your face. And then I'll take care of him myself."

Stacia laughed at the thought. She opened the door and hopped out. "Bye, Mom!"

Reena leaned over so should could look Stacia in the eye. "Bye," she said. "And yeah, he probably likes you. But I love you."

Stacia gave her a huge smile and said, "I love you, too! Bye!"

Reena waved, and then teared up a bit as her little girl jogged away. "Oh my God. I'm so unprepared for all of this. Today better be a drama-free day at work."

After wiping her eyes, Reena pulled away from school and sped off towards the Home.

On the other side of town, JB pulled open his door and peeked out. When the coast was clear, he slipped out, wearing bright orange swim trunks and a white towel around his neck. Just like the previous morning, he tiptoed around the hall and knocked on exactly three doors. Marvin, then Nelly, then... slowly... Abe all peeked out their doors. The three of them wore swimsuits and towels as well.

JB and his three friends crept down the hall in the opposite direction of the nurse station. Right before they turned down a narrow corridor, JB glanced behind them and saw two men in gray suits walking into Powell's office.

"Hmm," he said. "That doesn't look good."

But today's adventure couldn't wait. He led Abe, Marvin, and Nelly down the darkened corridor to a door marked: THERAPY POOL - CLOSED FOR RENOVATION.

JB opened the door with a flourish and held it open for his three accomplices. The sharp tang of chlorine filled his nose, along with a whiff of mildew.

Nelly paused before entering. "Are you sure about this, JB?" she asked.

"Positive. Peterson said they just had the pool cleaned last week. Now that he's officially trained up, Bart's gonna start pool therapy soon. So we're just getting a jump on the crowd."

Nelly smiled and stepped inside. Marvin was already at the pool's edge, clapping with joy. His clapping and their voices echoed inside the shadowy pool area.

"This place is amazing!" Marvin shouted.

JB quivered with excitement as he waited for Abe to roll his walker down the corridor to the entrance.

"Come on, buddy," he called. "Come on come on come on." He helped Abe into the pool area, and then aimed him toward the far end. "There you go. I'll help you into the shallow end."

"Just don't... let Nelly jump in... before I get there..."

"I hear ya, Abe," JB said with a wink. "You sly dog."

Abe pulled up short and pointed a bony finger at JB. "Don't get the wrong idea, youngster. It's not like that. She's frail. I gotta keep an eye on her. Safety first. That's all."

"Um-*hmm*," JB said. "Weren't you the one telling me to knock her block off during the kickball game the other day?"

With a shrug, Abe squeaked and rolled past JB. "Don't recall that, sonny-boy..."

Marvin was already dog-paddling around the pool, which was a bit worse for the wear, but otherwise clean. JB felt waves of heat coming off the water, thanks to Peterson flipping the heat on yesterday. Nelly sat with her toes in the shallow end, smiling with anticipation as she pulled a red swimming cap over her short white hair.

JB hurried around the tiled pool walkway, pulling up window shades and flooding the big room with morning light.

"This is so awesome," he said to anyone who would listen. "And to think I'd never even *know* about this place if Peterson hadn't told me last week. See what doing favors for people will do for you?"

Abe frowned at JB, suddenly apprehensive as he inched closer to the pool, holding onto his walker with one hand. When he dipped a toe into the warm water, though, he almost smiled. JB pretended not to see.

Marvin splashed at JB and went under another time, leaving just his big feet kicking in the air.

Nelly finally slipped into the water with a soft splash. "Amazing," she said when she popped back up. "Like bath water."

JB couldn't stand it any longer. After raising the last window shade, he threw down his towel and leapt into the deep end. "Cannonball!" he cried, followed by a gigantic splash.

For the rest of the morning, the whole world existed only in the Whispering Pines swimming pool. Nelly swam slow, graceful laps across the pool, a huge smile on her face every time she came up for air. Marvin floated into the deep end, doing the back float and squirting water out of his mouth like a fountain. Even Abe got in up to his neck in the shallow water, grinning at JB and Nelly, but mostly Nelly.

And JB kept running and jumping into the water, one cannonball after another.

Finally, a bit worn out but grinning, JB swam over to the others. They all converged around Abe in the shallow end.

"So," he panted. "What do you guys think? We've gotta get Powell to spring for a diving board next."

Marvin splashed at JB again, chuckling. "I'm not sure that a bunch of old folks should be going off a *diving* board, JB. There's probably rules about that."

Nelly floated off, gazing at the door leading to the rest of the Home.

"I wonder," she said, "when the others are going to show up."

JB nearly fell over in surprise. "The *others*?" he said.

"Well, yeah," Nelly said. "I told some friends about the pool last night at dinner. I guess they're sleeping in. Or maybe they don't have bathing suits."

"Oh. Hmm," JB said, feeling a sudden sense of panic. "I'm not sure about all that. I don't want this to get out of control..." He looked at the clock on the wall, but its second hand wasn't moving. He had no idea what time it was, or how long they'd been there. "You know, we should probably head back to our rooms, too. Before Reena and the others—"

Abe's harsh laugh interrupted JB. He pointed at the door.

"Looks like the word got out after all," Abe said.

First two, then three, then half a dozen more residents filed through the door in bathing suits, carrying towels. It was everyone from the kickball game and then some more.

JB's eyes went wide for a moment, and then he nodded and grinned.

"Yeah," he said. "*Yeah!* This is gonna be great. A day to remember, for all of us."

Within minutes, the pool area was filled with even more splashing and shouting as the other old folks jumped, stepped, or eased their way into the water.

JB's smile faded a tiny bit when he watched Nelly rubbing her temple, as if she had a migraine. He scurried through the water next to her again.

"Everything okay, Nelly?"

"Oh," she said, surprised at his sudden presence next to her. "I'm fine. Just a bit of a headache."

JB waved at all the other folks swimming around them. "Hey, nice work, Nels. You're right. This is an experience to be shared by everyone. I'm glad you got the word out."

"Thank *you*, JB," Nelly said. "You've been a, well. A life saver."

JB blushed and ducked his head under the water for a second. Nelly was still there, grinning at him, when he resurfaced.

"Ah, go on," he said. "I just wanted everyone to get out of their rut. This place was so dull and quiet when I first got here."

"No kidding. I thought I was going nuts, and I'd only been here a year when you arrived."

JB turned his gaze away, feeling suddenly troubled. As if a memory was trying to shake itself loose in his mind. "Yeah," he said, thinking of the picture he kept closed up in his desk. "Only a *year...*"

Nelly splashed him, knocking him out of his reverie.

"We should probably get everyone back to their rooms, shouldn't we?"

"Yeah," JB said. "You're right. It's getting a little late. It's probably close to lunch time."

"But first," Nelly said, heading for the side of the pool. "Watch *this*, young man."

Nelly pulled herself out of the water and stood up straight at the edge. She paused, rubbed her right temple again just for a moment, and then tucked a loose hair under her red swim cap. She raised her thin arms above her head.

JB grinned at her, and everyone else stopped to watch. The entire pool area went silent.

Bathed in mid-day sunlight from the windows, Nelly smiled at her audience. She went up on her toes and leaped forward— a perfect swan dive, with barely a splash as she cut through the water.

The place erupted in cheers that echoed off the walls and ceiling. JB splashed Abe and hollered as loud as he could.

Everyone was back in the water again again when a shadow filled the doorway. It was Bart.

"All right!" the big man boomed. "Everyone *out!*"

"I knew it," Abe muttered next to JB. "Too good to last."

JB took Abe by the arm and was about to lead the old man out of the pool when he remembered Nelly.

She hadn't resurfaced.

JB saw Nelly's red swimming cap floating in the middle of the pool. He let go of Abe and looked around at all the people leaving the pool, but he didn't see her in the crowd.

For a painful moment, JB's eyes met the furious eyes of Bart from across the pool.

Then Bart was diving into the water, aiming his big body at Nelly's cap and the shape five feet under it.

The pool area erupted again, this time in screams and the wild thrashings of panic. JB pushed his way through the water toward the cap as well, as if this was some kind of terrible race, without a winner.

And even as he struggled to get to Nelly, JB knew that it was already too late.

* * * * *

L ying with his head at the foot of his bed, JB realized that he'd never looked out the window of his room this way before. He'd spent the past six months with his blinds closed tight and his back to the window. Now he stared at the sun trying to peek out from the gray clouds. As he watched, a tear slipped from one eye and slid untouched down his cheek.

He looked down at his hands. They were both shaking.

Today had stirred up too many bad memories. And he knew the next few days would not get any easier.

Tired of being alone and staring at the clouds, JB finally left his room and crept over to Amelia's room.

The little black woman remained dwarfed by her machines, in the exact same position as when JB checked on her yesterday. Every day he had to stop by, at least once. Just in case.

He saw her chest rise, just the tiniest bit, and he exhaled in relief and wiped at his eyes, which had filled with tears without his awareness or his permission.

When he cleared his vision, he could have sworn that he saw Miss Amelia twitch her left shoulder.

He moved closer, until he was almost hovering above her. He watched her, unable to believe what he'd just seen, anxious to see if it would happen again.

"Miss Amelia," he finally said in a hoarse voice.

But she remained motionless. Barely breathing.

JB swallowed and exhaled. "Hang in there, Miss Amelia," he whispered on his way out the door.

Farther up the hallway, JB saw the two men in suits again, along with a woman in a gray pants suit, standing just outside of Powell's office. They were talking together in low voices, and they didn't see JB.

Powell emerged from his office and hurriedly shook hands with each of them. The drab-suited trio departed. JB crept closer, hoping to overhear something about the three suits, who were most likely inspectors.

Terrible timing for a surprise inspection, JB thought.

He watched Powell nod at LaTanya and Megan at the nurse station, and then he stagger into his office, closing the door behind him.

JB padded up the hall and slipped through the door to the kitchen, in dire need of some fresh air. But when he arrived at the loading dock, the spot was already occupied.

Reena sat on the edge of the loading dock with an unlit cigarette in her shaking hand. It was cold out here. JB wanted to turn around, but it was too late for that.

Reena turned when she heard his approach. She gave JB a tired smile, and then she shook her head.

"I'm so stupid," she said, "I bought another pack on my way back from the hospital, but I forgot to get matches. My daughter threw away my lighter."

JB looked at her with dead eyes, just for a moment, terrified that she would be beyond furious with him for what had happened today. He carefully sat down beside her, leaving a good three feet between them.

"Probably for the best?" he said, nodding at the cigarette.

"I guess. I just could use... *something*. The ride to the hospital with her, and after we got there... It was pretty awful."

JB winced.

"I bet." He took a quick breath and swallowed. "Nelly would've liked it that you were there with her, I think."

Reena tucked the cigarette back into the pack and then threw the pack into the dumpster next to them. "The doctors said the stroke was massive," she said. "She wouldn't have felt a thing."

"Oh man," JB said, shaking from the cold. "A stroke. You warned me about that. I *did* kill her with my God damn shenanigans."

Reena's eyes hardened, just for a moment, as if she might have agreed with that theory. And then she shook her head.

"No. You can't think like that. You just never know, JB. We all thought her heart condition would be the cause. We were wrong. You just can't know. So do *not* beat yourself up. Got it?"

"But if we hadn't snuck off to the pool—"

"—Then she would have died in her sleep. Or at dinner. And she never would've gotten to go swimming one last time."

JB looked up sharply at that, utterly surprised. "You really mean that? You're not just saying that?"

Reena nodded.

JB gazed at the sun starting to set over the city. He felt like he could either laugh or cry.

"The family's set up the wake for tomorrow," Reena said. "Think you'll be able to make it? I don't know if it'll bring up any bad memories..."

JB flinched at the word. Then he tried to cover it up with confidence, saying, "Oh no, I've got to go." He exhaled a plume of warm air into the cold night. "It's *tomorrow* already?"

"I guess the family just wanted to get it over and done with. I don't think they were very close."

JB felt suddenly very restless and vulnerable sitting out here in the cold, talking about death. "Um-hmm," he said. "Well, I'd better go get my nice clothes ready."

Reena grabbed his hand. He was surprised by how strong her grip was.

"Hush. Just relax, okay?" She gave his hand a squeeze, and then let go. "Just stop for a minute here and watch the sun set. We don't have to be anywhere right now."

JB started to protest, and then he simply nodded. He gave one last glance at Reena, and she met his gaze. They both smiled. They leaned closer—just for warmth, JB told himself.

In silence, they watched the horizon turn red.

JB sits in a church, eyes dead, wearing a loose-fitting brown suit. His face is ruined by grief and sleeplessness.

Organ music plays around him, a dirge, growing slowly louder.

Around him are a few old people, but the crowd is growing fast. Soon the church is filled with mourners, and everyone is crying, overwhelmed with sadness.

JB is now sitting in the front row, looking small and alone. Everyone else is gone.

Slowly, as if it's the hardest movement he's ever made, JB turns his head to the left.

There in the aisle sits not one coffin, but two. And the second one is tiny, painfully small. A small child's coffin.

Flowers cover both coffins, and a stuffed pink bear is affixed to the arrangement on the smaller coffin.

Outside, the late-winter wind promised a cold rain. JB and two dozen other older residents of the Home left three vans and trudged back to the Home after Nelly's wake. Everyone was dressed up, and all of their faces were etched with grief. The wind blew dead leaves across the lawn and nearly knocked a few folks off the sidewalk.

JB, wearing a brown suit that doesn't fit him well, walked slowly at Abe's side, leading the frail old man up the walk. Abe's eyes were red from weeping.

"I wish I could've seen her one last time," Abe said.

JB nodded, but couldn't find the words to answer him. Just as he'd done all morning, he was remembering someone *other* than Nelly. Two other someones that he hadn't been able to think about for nearly a year now.

JB patted Abe gently on the old man's back and urged him on toward the entrance. Abe's walker creaked and scratched the sidewalk with every other step.

JB had figured that Powell would at least have the decency to meet them all on their way in. But the entrance was left unmanned. JB stepped out of the way and waited for the others to get inside out of the cold. The wind was picking up, and he felt a few drops of rain hit the back of his head.

As soon as JB followed the last person from the wake inside, he heard shouting inside Powell's office.

"You can't do this!" a deep voice shouted. JB realized it was Powell doing the yelling. "This is outside your—your jurisdiction!"

After sending the rest of the mourners on to their rooms, LaTanya hurried over to Reena, while Megan crept closer to Powell's door to eavesdrop.

"Reena," LaTanya said. "You won't believe this, but Miss Amelia—"

She was interrupted by Powell again.

"I can't believe this," he yelled. JB found himself creeping closer to the door, just like Megan.

Reena put a hand on LaTanya's shoulder. "What's wrong with Miss Amelia?

"You can't!" Powell shouted. "Not right now!"

"They're gonna fight in there!" Megan said, half giddy and half scared, just as the administrator's office door was ripped open.

Powell poked his head out and pointed right at JB.

"Mr. Beckwith. The inspectors would like to speak with you. *Now.*"

JB closed his eyes for a moment. When he opened them, they were as blank and lifeless. He knew why the inspectors were there. How it was all his fault.

JB nodded and entered the office like a walking dead man.

Sometime in the middle of the night, as if the universe was working overtime to balance out its scales, Miss Amelia woke from her hundred-day sleep.

JB was the first to hear of it, and he got up early to talk with her by himself. After all that time asleep, the little lady had a lot to say.

"I figured I just slept long enough, you know?" she said. "I had some more to do with this old body of mine. I think it was the good lord up above, saying, 'Hold it girl, you got a few more good ones in ya.'"

JB laughed. "Smart guy, that good lord up above!"

"Oh, but what I wouldn't do for good shot of bourbon after all that. It was rough on a person. My mouth is so durn dry."

"Wish I could help you, Miss Amelia, but I got nothing. I'm hooch-free."

Amelia smiled, and then suddenly pulled JB close. "I got to tell you something, son. It's good to be back. I feel so lucky to be *alive*. I was ready for it all to end, while I was... gone like that. I reckon I'd about had enough of that limbo. Like that purgatory my Catholic friends talk about. An in-between place. More like *no* place."

JB leaned closer, nodding tentatively.

"I tell you what. It's no place for a *living* person to be." She let go of where she'd grabbed JB by the collar of his shirt. "You know what I mean?"

JB was speechless. He sat back, taking in Amelia's words. Finally he nodded.

"*Yeah*," he said, thinking of Nelly and Reena and Marvin and all the others. "I know exactly what you mean, Miss Amelia."

JB looked up when he heard familiar footsteps in the hall. Reena hurried past, and then she pulled up with a loud squeak of her shoes. She backtracked into the doorway.

"Miss *Amelia*!" Reena said. "It's so good to see you again!"

"Here I am," Amelia said with a cackling laugh. "Back for round two."

Reena smiled. "That's fantastic. You know, your friend Mr. Beckwith here visited you nearly every day, checking on you."

JB made a face, embarrassed. Reena gave him a meaningful look.

"He never gave up hope," she said, stepping further into the room.

JB shrugged as Miss Amelia patted his arm, proud of him.

"Now, I'm very, very sorry to interrupt," Reena said, and JB cold hear the stress in her voice. "But something has come up, and I'd like to speak with JB, if I can borrow him for a moment."

Amelia waved her tiny twig of an arm at JB and Reena and reached for her TV remote.

"Sure," she said. "I got time and lots of soap operas to catch up on. See ya later, JB."

JB followed Reena out of the room, and his smile faded when he saw the look on Reena's face outside.

"What is it?" he said, his spirits sinking. "What happened?"

A nicely furnished living room, messy with toddler toys, Elmo dancing down "Sesame Street" on the TV.

JB works at his laptop on the couch while his wife Lisa rolls around on the floor with their two-year-old daughter Emma.

Emma toddles over to him and grabs his pants leg. JB gently removes her hand and lifts a finger as if to say "Just one more minute."

From the floor, Lisa gives him an exasperated look, as if he's always too busy to enjoy his family. JB meets her gaze and points at the screen of his laptop.

Then he sees Lisa and Emma dancing along with "Sesame Street" and he grins. He sets aside his laptop so he can go play with them. They roll around and laugh for a few minutes, and then his phone distracts him. He checks his texts, and Lisa punches his shoulder.

JB apologizes, and then uses his phone to take a picture of Lisa and baby Emma, both wearing huge smiles.

It's the same picture he'll frame later. In a silver frame.

JB now held that framed photo of his wife and daughter tightly in his hand as he sat at the edge of the pool. The water was gone, drained from the pool in the two days since Nelly's fatal dive.

He tucked the frame into his big brown jacket as he got to his feet. Behind him sat a large duffel bag—a bag containing all his clothes and his meager other belongings.

JB was moving out.

For now, he left the bag behind and climbed down into the empty pool. His footsteps echoed as he walked carefully to the center on the slick, smooth surface. He could hear Nelly's voice with each step he took on the pool floor.

"This place was so dull and quiet when I first got here."

"Thank *you*, JB. You've been a life saver."

"But first. Watch *this*, young man."

He stopped at the spot where Nelly had nailed her dive. He looked straight up and pointed at the ceiling, eyes filling with tears of sadness as well as gratitude.

"No," he said. "Thank *you*. Thank all of you for saving *my* life."

Patting the picture tucked inside his coat pocket, JB carried his bag to the nurse station for what would be the last time. LaTanya and Reena heard him coming, and they stood up in unison, shocked. Megan peeked out from her desk, earbuds in as usual. She grimaced at JB and then disappeared again.

"Mr. Beckwith..." LaTanya began.

"JB," Reena said when her fellow nurse ran out of words. "You still have almost two weeks to get things settled and find another place. Just like all the other residents. You don't have to leave right now."

JB tapped the hard edge of the picture frame inside his coat pocket. "Don't you think," he said, in a not unfriendly way, "that it's way past time for me to go?"

"Look," LaTanya said. "It's not your fault they're closing us down, Mr. Beckwith. It was Powell's shady dealings, selling off the residents' private information to the highest bidder. Not anything you did." She paused. "Though you *did* do some crazy stuff."

"Thanks," JB said. "But I think my being here raised too many red flags. I hope you all are able to find new jobs, fast. I'm sorry for all this."

Reena nodded, her eyes filling with tears. She touched her wet eyes as if surprised. A phone rang, and LaTanya stepped back to answer it.

"This week," Reena said, shaking her head. "It's been the craziest week of my life."

JB reached over and caught a tear on her right cheek. It was surprisingly warm. Reena didn't even flinch away at his touch.

"I've had crazier," he said. "Unfortunately."

He set a key down on the desk in front of Reena.

"To my room. Although you and Bart already have a copy."

Reena let out an exasperated sigh. "You're really going, right now?"

"Yep." JB held out a hand, and they shook like strangers. "Thanks, Reena. For everything. You too, LaTanya. And Megan, if you can hear me."

Still on the phone, LaTanya leaned back out of her cube.

"Bye, Mr. Beckwith," she said, covering the mouthpiece. "You take care."

"Bye," Megan said faintly from somewhere in the other cubicle.

JB grinned at that and shifted the weight of his bag on his shoulder. "There you go. I know you'll all miss me badly. But I'm outta here."

With a final wave and a quick look down the hall towards the rooms where his friends would be forced to leave soon, JB walked out of the Home.

Outside, the late-winter wind pelted him with dead leaves and a stray plastic bag on his way to the street. The sun kept trying to break free of the clouds, but the clouds were more persistent.

He stood there in the cold next to the parking lot with his eyes closed and the wind blowing right in his face. He was smiling.

This was good, he told himself. Nelly's life and her death taught me something. As did everyone else here at the Home.

He gently took the framed picture out from inside his coat.

Before he could look at it, though, a small car rumbled up next to him. It was Reena. She cranked down her passenger window and waved at JB.

"Where to?" she called.

It took JB a second to figure out what she was doing there.

"Oh, hey," he said. "That's fine. I called a taxi. But thanks for the offer."

"JB. *Get* your ass in the car."

JB jumped at that, and then grinned. "Yes, ma'am!"

He set his bag in the back and dropped into her passenger seat. The little car squeaked and wobbled in response. Reena laughed.

"I can't let you leave the Whispering Pines Rest Home in a *taxi*. Not after all the good deeds you did there."

"*Mostly* good deeds..."

"*All* good. At least done with the best of intentions. Give yourself credit, Mr. Beckwith."

"Even if I did help get the place closed down?"

Reena smacked his shoulder in a friendly way.

"That was Mr. Powell's doing. The inspectors only started checking the finances when someone tipped them off about you staying here." Her face grew serious. "That wasn't *me*, by the way. Although there were days when I was tempted to do something like that. Before I understood what you were doing at the Home."

JB was utterly confused.

"Why are you so... *nice* about all this?" he asked. "You seem almost happy that the place is closing. You're gonna be out of a job in two weeks, you know."

Reena considered this, hand on her chin.

"Maybe, in a way, I *am* glad. I'm sad that all the clients— residents—will have to be uprooted and moved somewhere else. And I'll miss all of you. But I think I was starting to feel stuck in a rut there."

"They call it... *limbo*," JB said in a surprised voice. Miss Amelia had been right on the money. "Or purgatory, sometimes."

"Yeah," Reena said, reaching across to touch the framed picture in JB's hand. "Exactly."

JB couldn't help but pull the frame closer to him, keeping the back of it facing her, hiding the picture. Reena rested her hand on JB's hand instead.

JB barely noticed her touch as he gazed out at the Home.

"Some amazing memories there at Whispering Pines. I still stand by my original feeling. We were *lucky* to spend part of our lives there. Even if it was time spent in limbo."

He looked down at the framed picture in his hand, and then at Reena. With an effort, JB held up the frame and showed the photograph to Reena. That act just might have been the hardest thing he'd done in a long time, if not his entire life.

"You're the first person," he whispered, "that I've showed this to here."

"JB," she said, "I... "

"Reena, this is my wife Lisa, and our baby girl Emma. They were the lights of my life." He takes a sharp breath, and his hands start shaking. "And I lost them."

As Reena looked at the picture, she reached out and took JB's free hand in hers.

"They're beautiful," she said. "Thank you. Thank you for showing them to me."

JB squeezed her hand with his right hand, while his left clung to his picture frame. He let out a long, heartbroken sob that had been pent up for almost a year. It had felt like forever.

"It *hurts*. It hurts to remember them." Tears spilled down his face as he spoke. "But it does so much more damage to *not* remember them, you know? I see that now."

"So maybe your time at the Home wasn't all for nothing. Maybe it's just what you needed."

JB wiped his wet cheeks and considered this. "You sure you don't want to go back to school to be a psychologist instead of a PA, Reena? You're *good*."

Reena burst out laughing. "Only if you cover my tuition."

"I do need another place to invest my money now," JB said with a hesitant laugh of his own in spite of his tears, "now that the Home is closing."

Reena put her car in gear.

"Don't be crazy," she said. "What you *can* do is buy me lunch. And then we can take it from there."

JB gave Reena a long, meaningful look, still holding tight to her hand.

"*Deal*," he said, and as he spoke, something broke loose deep inside his chest, and he could breathe deeply again for the first time in a long, long while. "We'll take it from there, then."

Reena's car pulled away from the Home with a soft mutter. As she drove, the wind picked up and sent more dead leaves and bits of garbage flying behind the car. A ray of bright early-spring sun cut through the trees, hiding the car for a few moments with its pure brilliance.

When the sunlight faded and the wind calmed down again, the street was empty. Reena's car, with her and JB inside it, was gone.

About the Author

Michael Jasper loves to explore the places where the normal meets the strange. In pursuit of this fascination, he has written and published over a dozen novels, three story collections, sixty short stories, and a digital comic with artist Niki Smith.

In the past he attempted bartending, teaching junior high, painting houses, being a secret shopper, working construction, and many more jobs; he prefers fiction writing. For his day job, he works as a technical writer.

He lives with his family in North Carolina, and his website is **michaeljasper.net**.

www.ingramcontent.com/pod-product-compliance
Lightning Source LLC
Chambersburg PA
CBHW020558130626
46552CB00007B/2949